FLASH 52

FLASH 52

FLASH FICTION

Börkur Sigurbjörnsson

URBAN VOLCANO

Flash 52
Börkur Sigurbjörnsson

Creative Commons (BY-NC-ND) – 2017
http://creativecommons.org/licenses/by-nc-nd/3.0/

Cover: Ana Piñeyro
Illustrations: Börkur Sigurbjörnsson
Publisher: Urban Volcano

http://urbanvolcano.net/

ISBN 978-9935-9337-4-4

Contents

Good morning

"Good morning," said Laura and smiled toward the first wave of people flowing out of the train and up the stairs, heading for the next platform.

"Good morning," said Laura to the ocean of commuters passing her — a majority with a downcast gaze and concentrated on getting to work as quickly as possible.

"Good morning," said Laura to the silent mass that was scarcely talkative in the early hours of the day.

"Good morning," said a young woman walking slowly behind the crowd with her head held high.

"Good morning," said Laura. "I hope you'll have a lovely day."

Laura watched the woman disappear up the stairs. She got paid for greeting the morning traffic but considered it a nice bonus when a volunteer replied to her salute. She enjoyed the moment while waiting for the next train to arrive — due in one minute.

Jasmine

I watered the jasmine plant in the bedroom. I knew it very well that the plant was completely dehydrated and had been dead for quite a while. Yet, I could not bring myself to leaving it alone unwatered. There was something within me that told me I couldn't discriminate against some of my plants. Even if they were dead.

Point of view

Elizabeth looked up from the book. She was annoyed. The author irritated her. She could not stand his selective statistics to prove a point that wasn't that straightforward. Or his unsupported claims. Or his endless name-calling of his political opponents.

She would have stopped reading if it wasn't for the fact that the book had a good premise. Many of the arguments were appealing, albeit presented in an ill-supported vulgar way. The author was rightfully angry but could have done well to contain his anger.

Before returning to the book, Elizabeth had an idea. Why couldn't she just savor the book at its real value? She should simply enjoy the text as it was — a ranting-spree of an angry middle-aged man. She should write-off her expectation of an intellectual argumentation and enjoy the emotional roller coaster ride the author provided.

Elizabeth continued the reading, laughed out loud and enjoyed the book as never before.

Blindness

I turned the last page and put the book away. I had thoroughly enjoyed José Saramago's *Blindness*. It had been a while since I had immersed myself so deeply into a plot. For years I had never felt such an empathy for the characters. I was one of them.

I looked around me in the living room. Everything was white, uniformly creamy white. I didn't know on which page it had happened, but it had happened. I had myself become blind.

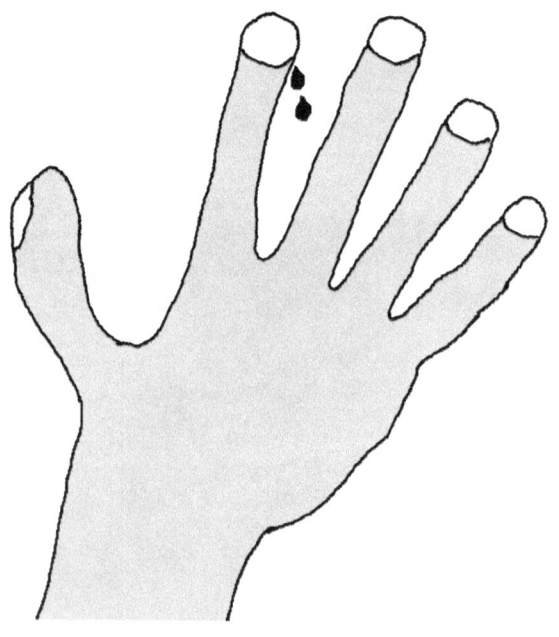

Nail-bite

Dennis glanced at his watch for the 30th time in the past 5 minutes. Now it was finally time for his meeting with the investors. They would call him into their offices at any time now. Dennis looked about the waiting room to see if there were any signs of his hosts. All he saw was the receptionist, deeply concentrated in staring at his monitor.

Dennis bit the nail of his right index finger. He ran his thumb over the nail to wipe off any traces of saliva. He came across a piece of loose skin that irritated him. He bit it off and felt the taste of iron on his lips. He pressed his middle finger against the index finger to try to stop the bleeding. In vain. The wound was too big.

"Dennis Newman!" the receptionist announced from the other side of the waiting room. "They are ready to see you now."

Get a life!

"Get a life!" you shouted, slamming the door behind you. I did not really understand what you were trying to say. I mean — I had reached level 247 and had 84 extra lives. I mean — how can you improve on that?

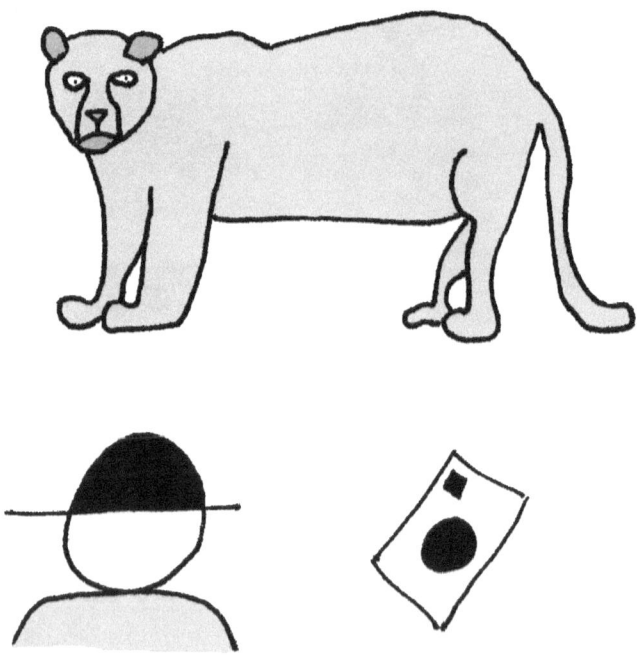

Freedom

We drove across the wetlands south of the Brazilian rainforest — driver, guide and four tourists. We gazed in all directions, looking for the big prize.

"Shhh," said the guide all of a sudden and pointed into the distance. We followed his indication down the river and over to the opposite bank. The driver slowed down and drove carefully downstream along the riverbank.

I grabbed my camera and pointed the lens across the river. The jeep stopped and I snapped. I let the camera sink and looked into the eyes of the big cat — the jaguar — that stood gracefully on the other side of the river.

I took a deep breath and felt a feeling of freedom rush through my body. This was exactly what I had had in mind when I decided a month ago to quit my job, travel the world and seek adventure.

Walking against the flow

As I listened to more presentations about how we could improve our urban wellbeing, the more I felt myself as an alien in this world.

When the world believes in a future of self-driving cars, I dream of a future of self-walking humans. When the world is excited about installing sensors for smart parking, I think of walking as the smartest parking solution.

When the world starts debating technology as humanity's savior, I go for a walk in the park.

Energy transfer

I walked out of the office building after a full day of meetings. I was mentally exhausted, but craving for physical activity. I needed to release some of the static energy that had been building up in my body during the day and turn it into mental energy. Rather than going directly to the nearest underground station and taking the first train home, I decided to walk to a station further downstream along the route.

As I walked through the park across the street from the office, I could feel the fresh breeze rinsing my lungs of the stale meeting-room air. I enjoyed watching the squirrels run and listening to the birds tweet. When I reached the street on the other side of the park, my shoulder muscles relaxed, I straightened my back, lifted my head and started a mindful observation of the world around me.

After one sweep across my surroundings, I felt a knot in my stomach. My mind jumped to last week's terrorist attacks. My brain started racing. Was it safe to be in the streets? Was I doing a stupid thing? Was it a folly to take such an unnecessary risk? Was I insane to deliberately expose myself to the terrorists — to their vans, knives and explosives?

I felt my muscles stiffen, my heart beat faster, my breathing become shallow. I distrusted people with backpacks. I felt wary of white vans. I feared crossing the street. My mindful observation was replaced by paranoiac scrutiny. I turned around and rushed as fast as I could to the nearest underground station.

Purpose of fiction

"I have completely stopped reading works of fiction," said my colleague as the conversation moved on to the topic of reading. "I mean. What is the purpose?"

I contemplated if I should express my view that it was indeed the lack of purpose that made works of fiction so interesting and enjoyable. In the end I decided to just nod my head and smile. It was much more interesting to debate the topic with myself in my mind rather than trying to sow creative seeds in the infertile mind of my über-rational colleague.

Köningsegg

I walked over to the sink to wash my hands. I looked in the mirror and smiled politely at the reflection of the man who stood at the next sink.

"Are you in the car business?" the reflection asked.

"No," I answered, hesitating a little since I did not know exactly what he meant by "you." I did not know everyone who was at our table in the club, but I was pretty sure none was in the automotive industry.

"He does look quite like Köningsegg — the bold guy," said the man. "And you look like his chief engineer."

"I'm sorry," I said as I dried my hands on a mini-towel. "You are confusing us with others."

We walked together back into the dining hall and I wondered that it was a nice change to be confused with some other celebrity than Jürgen Klopp.

Waves

I lie on my back with my arms spread. It is partially cloudy but comfortably warm. The sea under me and all around is lukewarm but refreshing. The ocean waves alternate between lifting me up and pulling me down. The time stands still. I empty my mind. My only sensation is how my body oscillates up and down to the rhythm of the waves.

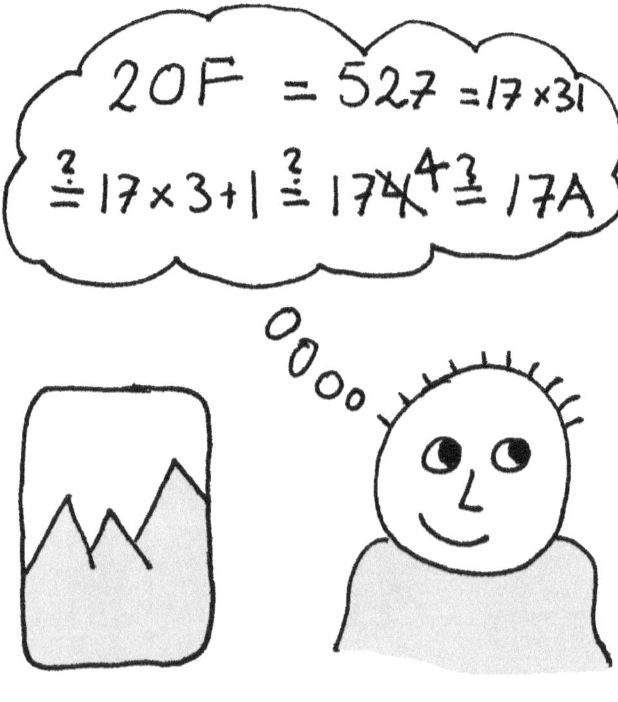
20F = 527 = 17×31
≟ 17×3+1 ≟ 17^4 ≟ 17A

"A window seat," I answered when the man at the check-in counter asked if I wanted to sit by the window or the aisle.

"I have 17A," the man said. "How does that sound?"

"That is impossible," I replied. "I cannot be in an A-seat. I cannot watch over the ocean when we come in for landing. I need to see land. I cannot imagine the descend into the ocean. Don't you have any F-seat available."

"Yes," replied the man. "20F is free."

"20F," I echoed. "That is 527 in the hexadecimal system. 17 times 31. 17 times 3 plus 1 is 17 times 4. 174. Which is more or less like 17A. Almost exactly the same seat as you offered me in the beginning!"

"Excuse me?" asked the man. "Does that not suit you either?"

"But, yes," I replied. "Don't be silly. Of course that suits me."

Nodding heads

By the coffee machine I met a man. We nodded our heads as to acknowledge each other's existence. We had ran into one another quite regularly over the past couple of weeks and always greeted with a nod.

I knew I had spoken to this man at some point. However, I could not for the love of an atheist superhuman remember where it had taken place, when, or who the man was.

We stared at the ceiling in an awkward silence while the machine poured hot black liquid into his cup.

"Goodbye," he said when his cup was full.

"Goodbye," I replied, placing my cup under the faucet and pressing the espresso button.

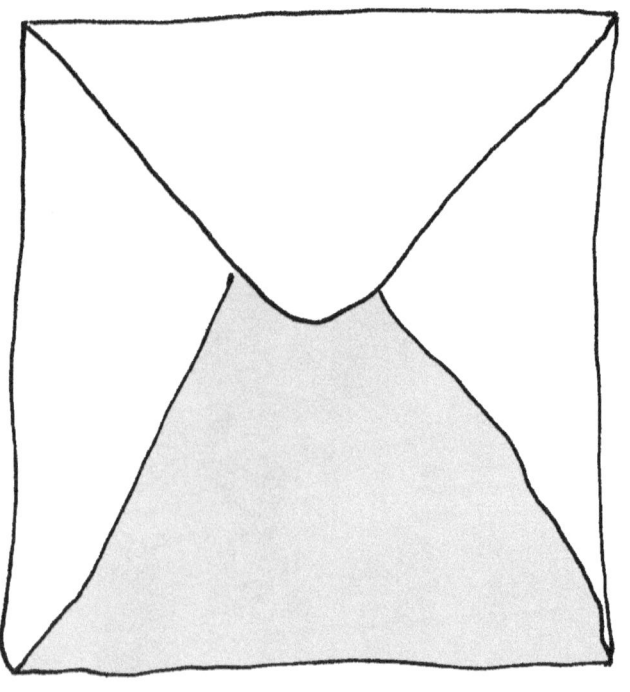

The letter

I walked into the storage room and looked over the pile of boxes. I knew that my university diploma was there somewhere — the proof that I had finished my masters degree in geology.

I opened the boxes one after another in search of the right folder. Luck was with me on the third box. I extracted the file and opened it carefully. Though not with enough care to avoid a letter falling on the floor. Putting the folder aside I reached for the yellowish envelope that was not addressed to anyone.

I pulled out a densely written paper and started to read. A smile came over my face as I read my own handwriting, explaining to my family and friends the reasons why I had decided not to finish my masters in geology — why I could not cope anymore.

I had completely forgotten about this letter. A letter that was never sent but allowed myself to calm the turmoil in my head. It helped me take a deep breath and focus on finishing my thesis.

Out of touch with virtual reality

I am completely out of touch with virtual reality. I like being out in nature with a paper notebook and an ink pen. No batteries required.

Protest

I sat down with a large carton and a marker. I wanted to write a powerful message to the world. I wanted to protest. But what was it that I was protesting? The state of society. But what about the state of society? I wanted to protest against the bankers. But what did I know about derivatives and financial engineering? I wanted to protest against politicians. But what did politicians do, really?

I was clueless. I felt powerless about not being able to articulate what I wanted to protest. The state of our society was so complex that I just knew that something was not right but I couldn't put my finger on what was wrong. But wasn't that the whole point?

I fastened my grip on the marker and wrote my message to the world: "I demand a simple society where people like me can know what to protest!"

Insomnia

At five o'clock in the morning I sit on the living room floor, enjoying listening to the silence. I hear an occasional car drive through the otherwise empty streets. At six o'clock the birds wake up and start tweeting. From seven o'clock the humans get out of bed, one after another, and the city comes to life. At eight o'clock I fall asleep.

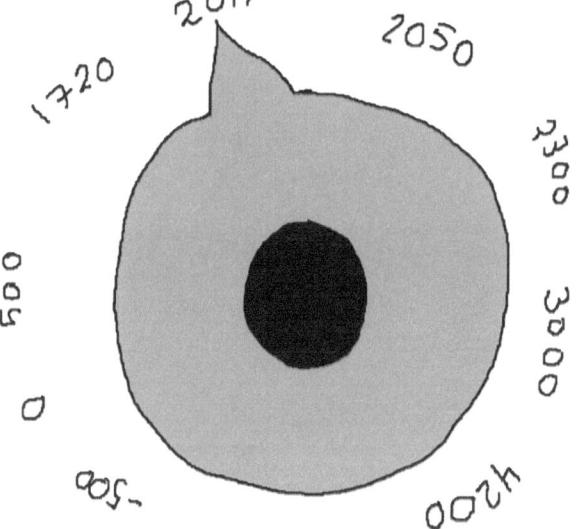

The time-machine

Billy fixed the last screw. His life was about to change for the better. During the forty-five years since he was born he had lived in the same boring town. In a place where truly nothing happened. Now, things were about to change. He had built a time-machine allowing him to travel back and forth in time to past and future glory-days of this place.

Billy took a seat in the time-machine and turned the dial forward 30 years — to 2047. There was a roaring noise for a moment until the machine calmed down again. Billy peaked out through the window and could see an aged image of himself swaying back and forth in a rocking chair besides a rusting piece of metal that looked a lot like his time-machine.

Disappointed with the lack of action Billy quickly turned the dial back to 1600. Again, there was a roaring noise before the calm. Billy stepped out of the time-machine and found himself in the middle of an uncultivated field. The sun burned in the sky and there was nothing to be seen except grass, as far as the eye could reach.

Billy spent the rest of the afternoon going back and forth in time, seeking exciting eras. He found none and came to the conclusion that this town was simply the most boring place on earth — independent of time.

After a few hours of time-travel he returned to 2017, grabbed a cold beer from the fridge and sat down in the rocking chair on his porch. He looked at the time-machine and said to himself: "I had to try."

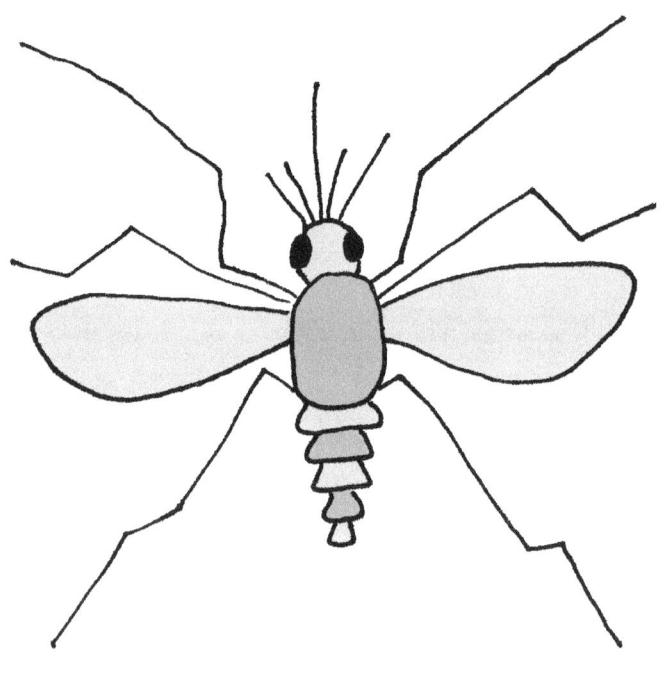

Blood revenge

I listened to the beast approach, smacked my arm with an open palm and left a trail of blood on both body-parts. I reached for a napkin and wiped off the red fluid.

I am generally speaking an animal friend, vegetarian and a member of various animal welfare charities. There is, however, something about killing mosquitos that gives me a great deal of pleasure. I call it blood revenge.

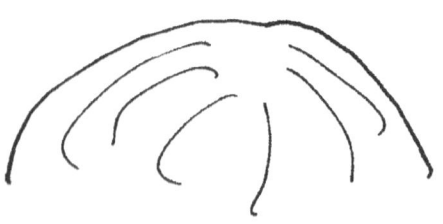

The secret book

I stepped into the subway car, took a seat and extracted Nabokov from my backpack. Before starting my reading I glanced over to the row of seats on the other side of the aisle.

Diagonally across from me sat at a young woman reading *Breakfast of Champions* by Kurt Vonnegut. My prejudices told me they were an odd couple, the lady and Kurt. The woman looked happy and full of joy. She would be a much better fit for *Breakfast at Tiffany's*.

Next to the woman sat a man reading *Mrs. Dalloway* by Virginia Woolf. A proper gentleman, it seemed, wearing a pin-striped suit and his hair combed back. He looked as if cut from a story about the English upper class. I smiled to myself as I imagined him as one of the guests in Mrs. Dalloway's dinner party.

I continued my scan along the row of seats and my glance stopped at a woman with a Kindle ebook reader. The smile disappeared from my lips. I did not like ebook readers. It destroyed my favorite pastime activity not being able to know what people were reading.

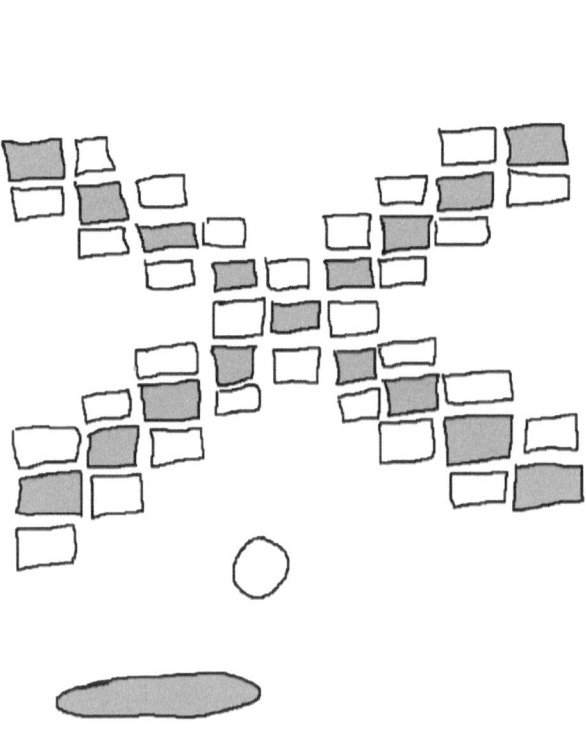

What do I think about when I think about life?

I was in a philosophical mood and decided to write an essay titled *What do I think about when I think about life?*

I started tackling the big questions. Why are we here? Why am I here? Why am I sitting here in an East London café drinking a decaf soy milk caramelized latte?

Then Steve walked past the table and I lost my train of thought. He's got this amazingly awesome retro eighties watch where you can play video games. I asked him to join me. I really wanted to play.

To sit on one's inner child

When the highly regarded speaker had finished his lecture I felt the urge to make a comment. What he had said made no sense — his presentation had been completely void of content. He had obviously lost touch with reality and was thoroughly locked up in his ivory tower.

I was about to raise my hand when I remembered that I had recently promised myself not to get involved in things that were none of my business. In this case it would be of little use to make a comment since it would most likely bounce off the arrogant speaker as water off a duck's back.

I restrained myself. As we say in Iceland, I sat on my inner child. Sometimes that makes life simpler.

Sharks

I cannot help smiling as I swim past the big glass window at the deep end of the pool. I think of the times I hardly dared swimming there due to fear that the window would burst open and out would swim a pack of man-eating sharks.

There are mixed feelings brewing in my mind as I think back at how hard it was to be a young boy with too wild imagination — terribly afraid of my own fictional creations.

The outer edge of the solar system

"I listened to an interesting show on the radio this morning," Jo-Anne said to Daniel as they sat on the sofa, sipping port after having put the girls to sleep. "They were asking people on the street how they would respond if offered a once in a lifetime one-way ticket to the outer edge of the solar system."

"And?" questioned Daniel without looking up from the gardening magazine he was reading. "How did they respond?"

"There were mixed reactions," Jo-Anne continued. "Some were really enthusiastic while some were really offended by the idea."

"I would be offended," said Daniel. "It's an indecent proposal."

"I can imagine," Jo-Anne said, smiling, gazing through the living room window at the line of trees marking the border of their garden. "I would go for it!"

"You would?" Daniel asked, putting the magazine aside on the sofa and looking directly at Jo-Anne. "What about me? The girls? And the roses?"

"Don't worry!" Jo-Anne said, looking Daniel in the eyes. "There are plenty of adorable single women out there who would love to become stepmothers to the girls — and the roses. But going to the outer edge of the solar system is a once in a lifetime opportunity."

Comfortable silence

The three of us sit together in the living room — my hosts and I — each in our own world. She reads a newspaper. He plays a video-game on his tablet. I write. Silence is in the foreground and a low-volume jazz in the background. Every now and then she tells us news from the paper. We listen, discuss and then go back to our own worlds.

Kathmandu and Kaiserslautern

"I read an interesting article in the newspaper this morning," Jo-Anne said to Daniel as they lay on the sandy Sardinian beach, drying themselves after their first Mediterranean bath of the day. "They were asking people on the street how they would respond if offered a once in a lifetime one-way ticket to the outer edge of the solar system."

"And?" questioned Daniel without looking up from the golfing magazine he was reading. "How did they respond?"

"There were mixed reactions," Jo-Anne continued. "Some were really enthusiastic while some were really offended by the idea."

"I can imagine," said Daniel. "It's an intriguing question. How would you respond?"

"I think I would pass," Jo-Anne said, smiling, gazing over the surface of the sea toward the horizon where it fused with the blue sky. "There are plenty of places on this earth I have yet to see. Like Kathmandu."

"Or Kaiserslautern, for that matter" Daniel added, putting the magazine aside on the towel and joining Jo-Anne's gaze at the horizon.

"Yeah!" Jo-Anne said. "Kathmandu and Kaiserslautern are truly examples of exotic places I would like to see before I head off to the outer edge of the solar system."

Death of a bullfighter

Yesterday, a bullfighter was stabbed to death by a bull in a small town in northern Spain. The incident took place in front of the village pub on the town's main square shortly before midnight, local time. The bullfighter was on his way home after having spent the evening at the pub, telling stories of his heroic acts in the bullring, when the bull attacked him from an ambush.

The bull escaped from the scene but was found later in the night in a field in the outskirts of the town. It is not known if the perpetrator and victim knew each other but there is suspicion that the crime was motivated as a revenge for the death of a close relative.

The doodle

The lecture was terribly boring so I entertained myself by doodling. I really enjoyed drawing, shaping patterns, animals, trees and people. I considered myself an artist even if I did not make a living from my work.

The world, however, was more hostile to my creations. This is not art, it said. This is vandalism, said the world, as if my shapes were an offense to humanity.

"Hey!" the man sitting in front of me in the lecture hall suddenly shouted. "You're drawing on my jacket!"

My point exactly. The world has no appreciation for the fine arts.

How are you?

How are you? you ask in a smooth voice with a sympathetic smile on your face.

Before you asked, I was fine. I was relaxed. I was enjoying myself. I had forgotten about my money troubles. I had forgotten about the time pressure. I had forgotten about the lawsuit. I was really fine.

Since you asked, I start thinking and my anxiety comes back with full force.

Downpour

I was speaking at a lunchtime meeting when it started to rain. The shower fell from the heaven as if poured from a bucket.

"Excuse me," I said and left the room.

I walked along the hallway, down the stairs, across the reception and out the main entrance until I came to a halt in the middle of the square outside the headquarters.

I stood still and let the rain bombard my head. I enjoyed feeling the water trickle down the sideburns, neck, chest, stomach, thighs, shins and all the way down to my toes.

After five minutes in the downpour I returned to the headquarters, through the main entrance, across the reception, up the stairs, along the hallway and toward the meeting room.

The meeting was in full swing with a lively debate that stopped as soon as I opened the door, walked to the stage with a torrent of water trailing me and took up the thread where I had left it.

Seeking monarch

Job tile

- Monarch

Essential qualities

- Born at the right time to the right parents.

Desired qualities

- Good table manners.

- Literacy is a plus.

We offer

- Unquestioned loyalty.

Chill

The door slammed with such a noise that it woke me up. I looked at the alarm clock on the bedside table. It was six. It had thus been a dream after all.

Even if it was a relatively warm summer morning, a chill went through my body. The dream had left me uneasy. I felt like an outsider.

I took a hot shower in order to try to get rid of the chilling feeling. I shivered under the warm stream.

"You're up early today," my wife said as I entered the kitchen. "What's the occasion?"

"I had a bad dream," I said with a blatant attempt at a fake smile. "I was at work. At first, my desk was below a leaking skylight. Then it was by an exit where cold air blew in as people came and went. I was frozen to the bone. My keyboard was rusty. I wandered around the office, trying to find a better place to work. All in vain."

"Honey, you need to start looking for a new job," my wife said. "This one is not for you."

The novel

I opened the notepad and started writing. The words jumped from the tip of my pen like blue-clad paratroopers out of the hatch of an airplane. The story flowed as a river in the spring-time. I felt good. I enjoyed sneaking into the world of the novel. I enjoyed submerging myself completely in a world where I had total control over the plot.

Chasing a dream

I open my eyes, look up at the ceiling and watch the lamp swing back and forth in the breeze entering through the open window. I had been dreaming. We were together on a vibrant square in a Mediterranean city. We talked, and you were about to tell me why you had left me — why you had disappeared from my life.

I close my eyes and return to the square. I look around, trying to find you. You are nowhere to be seen. The square is empty. I start running. I run up and down the side-streets around the square, looking for you. I need to find you. I need to know why you left me. I run up one street and then turn the corner into another. Just like the square, the streets are all empty. There is no one to be seen. The dream is gone.

I return to the square, panting after all the running. I lean forward, placing my hands on my knees and try to breathe normally. I know my chase is futile. I am never going to catch you. I give up, open my eyes and return to reality.

The sign

I regretted having asked God for a sign. I wasn't seeing things any clearer now than I had done before. I was just as confused. Maybe I still felt dizzy after being struck by a lightning, but I did not dare to ask God for further elaboration.

Museum of peace

A sensation of peace came over me as I entered the main exhibition hall of the museum. I could feel my breathing slow down and get deeper. I don't know much about art or artists. I cannot distinguish this-ism from that-ism, and I have never been praised for my sense of aesthetics. However, there is something about visiting museums that makes me relax. Maybe it is the big empty spaces. Maybe it is the leisurely stroll. Maybe it is because I stop thinking and just stare at the objects without judging them. I don't understand why I feel this way. I just do. And I like it.

Payback

I loved racing my bicycle down the hill. The sun reflected on my forehead and the wind played with the locks peeking down from under the helmet. I felt butterflies in my stomach because the speed was reaching the limit I could comfortably handle.

I was in the seventh heaven until it occurred to me that on my way home I would have to pay for this moment of joy by cycling back up the hill.

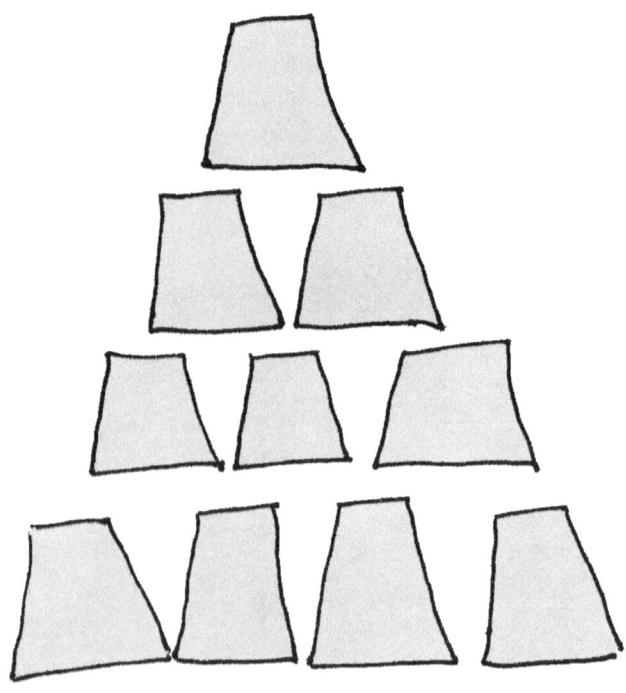

Playtime

I stacked plastic cups into a house-of-cards-like structure, punctured one cup with a hole punch, chained a few rubber bands together, threaded them through the holes and strapped the cup on my head like a cowboy hat. I looked at myself in the mirror, winked, shot my own reflection with the index finger and blew away the smoke. I was on fire.

I grabbed the rest of the rubber bands, took five steps away from the desk and started to shoot my ammunition at the stack of cups. I loved having my own private office. It was so much fun to be able to close the door and fool around when no one could see.

I had almost shot down all the cups when my play was interrupted by the intercom.

"Yes!" I said in the harsh voice I always use when I don't want to be disturbed.

"Mr. Prime Minister," said the intercom. "The Queen is on the line. She says it's urgent."

"I see," I sighed, pausing for a moment. "Ok, I'll take it."

Senses

Joseph stared at his friend who sat across the table and talked endlessly. He admired how the nostrils vibrated in tune with the words that came streaming from the mouth. Joseph enjoyed following how his friend's Adam's apple moved up and down like a buoy on a slightly troubled sea.

Joseph did not have a clue regarding what his friend was going on about. We are all born with differently sensitive senses. Joseph's sight was much more responsive than his hearing. Therefore, he chose to be around friends who talked much but whose speeches were void of content and did not necessarily need an audience.

The Norbert Peterson Tower

Norbert Peterson glided slowly upward from the underground, holding onto the handrail of the escalator. He was on his way to take his first peek at the completed construction of his first skyscraper. The KP-Energy Tower, or the Norbert Peterson Tower as his colleagues called it. It was the tower that could transform his career from being an architect to being a starchitect.

Once on the surface, Norbert's gaze hesitantly followed his design from bottom to top. He crossed the street to get a better angle. He walked backwards down the street with his eyes fixed on his creation.

Norbert shook his head. It did not work. It did not fit in. The building that had looked so good on paper in his studio simply did not scale to a full-size construction.

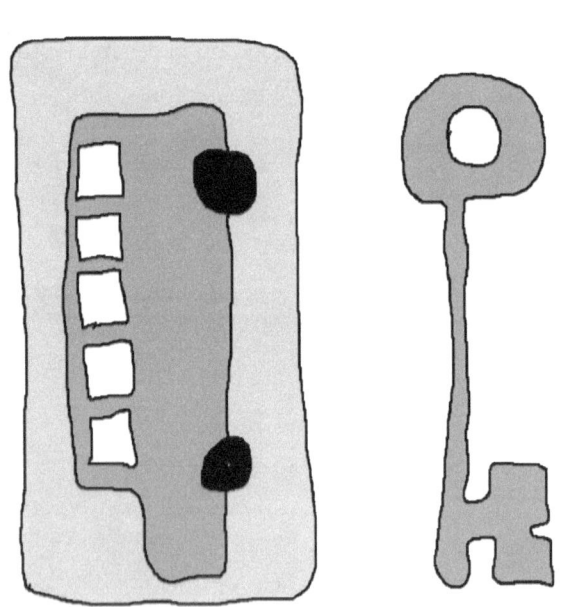

Something is not right

Victoria arrived at the front door of her house, mentally exhausted after a long and demanding day at the office. She took her Oyster card from her pocket and brought it to the keyhole. Her brain was too tired to act immediately but deep inside she knew that something was not right.

Friendly fire

As Pedro entered the train he noticed that it was unusually packed for the time of day. He looked about him and miraculously spotted a folding seat that was occupied by a backpack. As Pedro approached the seat, the backpack's owner, a young man in his late teens, looked up, smiled, removed his backpack and held the seat down for Pedro to sit.

"Thank you!" said Pedro, impressed by the politeness of the juvenile passenger. If only there were more like him in his generation. He was a shining exemplar.

The train started moving and Pedro made himself comfortable, took out his book and started to read. He really enjoyed being able to submerge himself in a good book on his way to work.

Pedro hadn't read many words when he was interrupted by a low murmur of gunshots, explosions, shouts and cries. Someone seemed to be playing a computer game or watching a movie on their mobile phone without using headphones. This was outrageous. How could anyone disrupt the nice and quiet mid-morning commute with such an inconsiderate behavior? He had to do something to stop this.

Pedro looked up from his book and found out to his horror that the noisemaker was the friendly juvenile who had kindly offered him a seat. He opened his mouth but said nothing. He could not bring himself to scolding this young man who had been so nice to him.

Superhuman

"Is it true?" you asked when I told you about the latest rumors that were flying about the cafeteria at lunchtime.

"As far as I know," I answered. "However, I cannot be hundred percent certain. I'm only human. I'm no historian."

"So, you consider historians as super-human creatures?"

"No," I replied. "It was just a figure of speech."

The body that cried

Robert felt a slight pain in the chest and a shortness of breath. Was it the heart? No, the pain was on the right side but the heart on the left. Or did that matter? He felt his heart beat faster. Was it really physical pain? Or was it psychological? A panic-attack? Was it muscular or musculoskeletal? Or something in-between?

Robert took a deep breath, looked out through the window and fixed his eyes on the distant mountains. The pain faded, his breathing stabilized and his heart returned to its normal beat.

Robert knew that listening to one's body is an important part of preventive medicine. He just wished that it could be more articulate about what it wanted to say.

Train story

I struggled with focusing on my reading, interrupted by a boy across the aisle who babbled on endlessly.

"Daddy," said the boy. "Are all the people going to London?"

"I don't know," answered the father.

"Daddy! How far is it to London by train?"

"Three hours."

"Daddy! If someone were too poor to pay the fare and had to walk to London, how long would it take?"

"A few days."

"Daddy! And when they arrived in London, would they be dead?"

"Yes," answered the father. "Dead-tired."

Rocks

I opened the suitcase and was confronted with a pile of sweaty t-shirts and shorts. I quickly scooped all the clothes into the laundry basket.

At the bottom of the suitcase I noticed the two small rocks I had collected on one of my walks about the island. I shook my head. Why did I insist on the idea that some day in the distant future I would refresh my high-school geology by analyzing rocks and minerals?

I opened the desk drawer and fetched two small ziplock bags. I put a rock into each bag and labelled them "Ibiza 2010". I opened the wardrobe and pulled out a heavy box. I placed the two rock samples in the box alongside hundreds of similar bags. I closed the box and deep inside I knew that I would never see these stones again.

The barber

Listen, said the barber as I sat down in his chair. I have been a barber for 30 years. I have had the hair of uncountable interesting personalities in my hands. I have heard all the stories that exist under the sun. I have had enough. I have no interest in knowing who you are, where you come from or what you are going to do this weekend. I am just going to keep my mouth shut and cut your hair. Understood?

The dog whisperer

After finishing our dinner at the farm hotel, we decided to take a stroll about the estate before returning to our room. We followed the gravel paths, arm in arm, through the pitch-black surroundings, gazing at the stars and drinking in the quiet night.

As we approached the staples, two small dogs came running toward us — barking their lungs out. I could feel both our bodies stiffen, our heartbeat quicken and we hesitated to continue our stroll down the road.

"Shhhh," I whispered into the direction from where the dogs came running and stretched out an arm with the palm open wide.

The dogs stopped running but took up a defensive position in the middle of the driveway in front of the stables — growling in our direction. While still tense, I could feel both our bodies relaxing a bit as the situation calmed.

"Wow, that was amazing," you said in a hushed tone after we had walked past the stables and turned on to a different path leading back toward the hotel. "How you managed to calm those dogs!"

"Eh," I admitted. "I wasn't really trying to calm the dogs."

"Oh," you said, burying your head in my chest. "So, you were calming me. Well, that worked too."

"I wasn't really trying to calm you either," I thought, but decided to keep to myself that my efforts were purely introverted.

The street cleaner

I meet him every morning on my way to the subway. He is there on the same street corner, sweeping and shoveling up heaps of fallen leaves. We greet each other. It is a pleasant part of the daily routine.

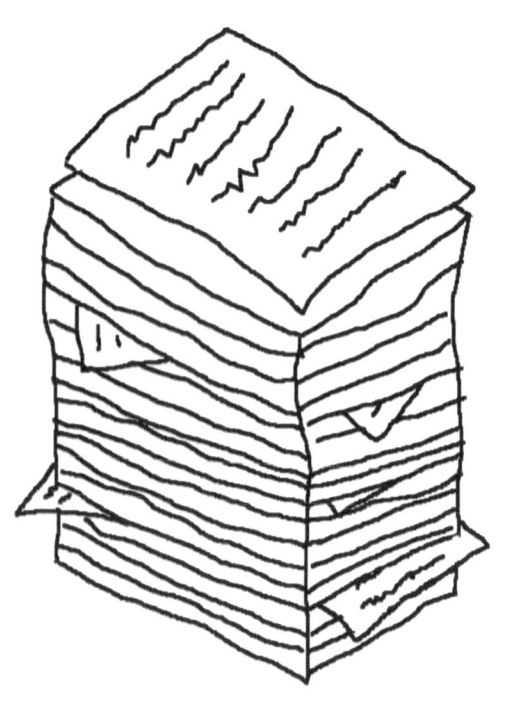

The autobiography

I put down the pen, turned the page and placed it on top of the ones that had come before it. The pile of paper was now the complete first draft of my autobiography. In my 40-years-long career as a writer I had never written so many lies. Never had I put so much fiction on paper. Yet, the autobiography was faithful and consistent with the perception I had portrayed over the years. True to the smoke and mirrors I had erected around my personal life.

The veracious account of my life was written in my novels. Fifteen best-selling works of make-believe fiction. The books that mainstream critics rejected as immoral and unrealistic, with seriously flawed characters. The same stories my readers acclaimed with perverse satisfaction. The accounts of a life that no one dared to admit they desired but everyone secretly craved.

That was my real life, but even I dared not confess.

Forward thinking

I lay in bed and thought about how my life had changed after I published my collection of flash fiction.

It had been a massive hit and sold a million and one copy. I used the money to make an old dream come true. I bought an old villa by the Mediterranean and spent my days between taking contemplative strolls on the beach and sitting on my balcony with a glass of wine in one hand and a pen in the other.

Deep inside I knew that my thoughts were nothing but a load of unrealistic nonsense. However, they allowed me to keep a positive outlook, lowered my stress-levels and helped me fall asleep.

Read more ...

More stories by Börkur Sigurbjörnsson can be found online:

http://urbanvolcano.net